Christina

Carole Kelly Moore

To order additional copies of this book, contact:
Xlibris
1-888-795-4274
www.Xlibris.com
Orders@Xlibris.com

ISBN: Softcover   978-1-7960-6828-3
        Hardcover   978-1-7960-6829-0
        EBook   978-1-7960-6827-6

Print information available on the last page

Rev. date: 11/21/2019

Christina

Chapter 1

Christina was born on a sunny day on the 21st of May. She was a lovely child with big brown eyes, thick curly black hair, and a small dimple in her chin. Grandma said said "What a fine child! We should call her Christina, after my mother." Because she was born in May, May became her middle name and her last name was Jackson from her father, Emmanuel Jackson, from the Jackson family of Atlanta.

The Jacksons were a family of sharecroppers from the deep south, and had been for for many generations until one day Grandpa Ben decided that they would do something else. So he moved them from Birmingham, Alabama to Selma, and they opened a small grocery store. Grandma Thelma ran the store after Grandpa Ben went to be with the lord, and her garden became a vegetable store. She shared her sweet, home-grown tomatoes with everyone in town and even won a blue ribbon at the local fair. They were soon called "Grandmas Homegrown Heirloom Supremes," and people came from far and wide to taste their juicy ripeness and to put them in salads. Everyone agreed, a greater salad you could not find anywhere.

Chapter 2

Life was good in the Jackson home. For Christina's fifth birthday, Grandma gave Christina a puppy. Grandma had told Christina that her first word was "lucky" so Christina decided to call her puppy that. He was white with black spots; a Dalmation, which is a firehouse dog. Grandma told Christina that Dalmatians' jobs are to rescue people and to keep keep the firemen company when they need to stay late in the firehouse. This made Christina feel very lucky indeed.

Chapter 3

"Hurry up Lucky, we can't be late! Ms. Smith needs us to be there on time!" It was Fireman Appreciation Day and Christina knew that Lucky needed to show support for his breed. Lucky must have felt it, because he was so excited his tail wagged extra fast that day. Christina was excited too. "Maybe he can ride in the fire truck," she thought as she buckled his red leash. Christina skipped down the street with Lucky until she approached the firehouse. "Hi Fireman Joe!" Christina called out when she reached the station. Christina always stopped at the firehouse on her way to school. She loved watching the men wash and shine the big red firetruck and it was always so exciting when they turned the lights on for her, and blasted the siren. "Hi Christina!" Joe called out. "Fireman Joe, it was my birthday and Grandma got me a puppy. I named him Lucky." "What a great name for a dog, Christina! I bet Lucky would like to meet our firehouse dog, Betsy." Fireman Joe whistled and Betsey the Dalmatian came running out. She liked Lucky, and the two wagged their tails and jumped up and down. At the end of the day everyone was happy. Lucky had a new friend and the children learn what to do in a fire. Christina went to bed that night thankful for the new friends she has made.

Chapter 4

"Today is a special day," Christina said to Lucky, "We can play in the yard until Grandma comes home from Mrs. O'Mara's house next door." Mrs. O'Mara was a nurse who worked in the local hospital in Selma. While she poured tea, she told Grandma about what she had seen earlier that day. "There was trouble on the bridge today," said Mrs. O'Mara, "Dr. King says we need to get organized to get the right to vote. The March didn't go well." Mrs. O'Mara took some biscuits out of the oven and put them on a big silver platter so that she and Grandma could have them on the front porch in the sunshine. Christina loved biscuits and came running over barefoot with Lucky when she smelled them in the air. "I hope everything will be alright..soon we shall know," said Grandma as she took a bite of the buttery biscuit. "Sweet child, there is going to be a cold spell tonight and I don't want you to get sick. Make sure to wear your woolen socks little miss!" "Yes, ma'am," said Christina and she grabbed a warm biscuit that she shared with Lucky. That night, Christina went to bed not knowing that history was being made right across the bridge near her home.

Chapter 5

Things were changing in Selma and Christina played her part.
She walked with the other children in what looked like a big
parade, but what Grandma said was a March. Her lumpy leg
had slowed her up so she could not finish The March, but
Grandma said that was ok. She has walked that day for the
right to vote, and any walking for that was good enough.
When The March was over, Christina went home to the best
fried chicken Grandma had ever made. Grandma always said
that hunger was the best spice. That night when Christina
went to bed, she felt proud. She said her good night prayers
as usual, but this time thanked Lucky, Grandma and everyone
else who walked with her on The March. Something about
that day had felt extra special.

Chapter 6

Christina was excited because there was going to be a spelling competition at school. The winner of the spelling bee would get to go to Washington D.C. Christina had never been away from home and this could be the chance of a lifetime. She could meet people who work with the President and change things about her town. Everyone has been talking about the Voting Act...maybe she could ask the President to help with that? Grandma always said to practice and don't ever give up, so that what she would do.

The day of the Spelling Bee the whole school was so excited that they were on the edge of their seats, and each time it was Christina's turn, she spelled another word correctly. If she won, she would be the best speller in the nation and get to go to Washington. Christina knew something magical was happening that day. She could feel it with every word she had remembered to spell.

Chapter 7

She won! …And the whole town showed up. At the train station they had balloons and signs posted "If Christina can't do it, no one can!" Another sign said, "This Is Just The Beginning!" It was all so exciting and Christina felt proud. Later, her Aunt told her that no one in the history of the Jackson family had ever been to the White House.

Chapter 8

Christina sat in what was called the White House Rose Garden. It was the most beautiful place she had ever seen with roses blooming everywhere. She wore a special lilac dress that Grandma had made just for her, and her hair was pulled back tightly in two braids. Mr. President approached her and held out his hand for her to shake. "Good job, Christina" he said and Christina smiled triumphantly. He gave her a gold medal and she thought about how she would keep it on her bookshelf for everyone to see. Christina was so happy that she decided to smile and shake everyones hand that day, like the President had done to her. It had made her feel so special. She even shook the cab drivers hand who dropped her and Grandma off at their hotel. This would be the first big journey of many to come.

Chapter 9

Aunt Caroline decided to come to Selma for a visit, and Christina could not wait. In Birmingham, Alabama where she was visiting from, Aunt Caroline was the most inviting person in town and everyone liked her. She had a bed and breakfast named Jackson's, and everyone was welcomed. If you didn't have enough money to stay the night, you could work in the kitchen for room and board. She didn't make a lot of money because she believed that her kitchen belonged to everyone and she would never turn people away. Aunt Caroline had heard about the Reverend King coming to Selma and she wanted to see him for herself. "I hope all goes well with The March," she told Grandma. Christina hoped so too. Christina could feel that there was change in the air.

Printed in the United States
By Bookmasters